Contents

STAR WARS

Qui-Gon Jinn

"Stay calm, we're not in trouble yet."

Qui-Gon Jinn is a distinguished elder of the Jedi Knights. Now in his sixties he is tall and imposing, with long greying hair.
Qui-Gon has all the qualities of nobility, wisdom, and leadership you'd expect to find in an accomplished Jedi Master. Yet he is still a wilful maverick who often prefers to follow his own chosen path!

Closely attuned to the living Force, Qui-Gon has a strong empathy for other living things. Though advancing in years, he remains an active and strong warrior. The sight of his powerful presence strikes fear into any enemy. Though he can never attack, but only protect. With his strength, knowledge, and patience, Qui-Gon is an inspiration to his headstrong apprentice, Obi-Wan Kenobi.

Together, they make a formidable team!

Every generation has a legend...

Every journey has a first step...

Every saga has a beginning...

My Book for the New Millennium

Name...
Address...
....
Planet...

Design and Layout by Simon Connor
Written by John Broadhead and Joyce McAleer

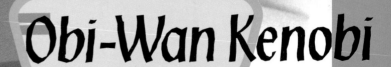

Obi-Wan Kenobi

"The boy's dangerous... they all sense it. Why can't you?"

Obi-Wan Kenobi is a worthy apprentice to Qui-Gon Jinn. Spirited, skilful, and strong-willed, he combines the noble qualities of the Jedi with the energy and enthusiasm of youth. Always quick and eager to impress his Master, Obi-Wan can also be headstrong, cocky, and a little naive, but is nevertheless a trustworthy and loyal companion.

While he is devoted to Qui-Gon and truly admires him, Obi-Wan doesn't always agree with his mentor's decisions. He gets frustrated with Qui-Gon's maverick tendencies, including his insistence on taking other life forms under his wing. Though still young, it's clear that Obi-Wan's natural inclination is to follow the rules. His training nearly completed, Obi-Wan is already a force to be reckoned with and he has the makings of a great Jedi Knight.

Nute Gunray

"Close the blast doors!"

A Nemoidian trade viceroy and the leader of the Trade Federation battleship, Nute Gunray takes his orders from his deadly master, Darth Sidious. Along with his fellow viceroy Rune Haako, he initiates a massive shipping blockade of the planet Naboo. Sly in character and ugly in appearance, Nute fears the Jedi and has a grudging respect for their power.

Rune Haako

"Have you ever encountered a Jedi Knight before, sir?"

Nute Gunray's comrade in aggression and cruelty, Rune Haako's position as a trade viceroy puts him at the forefront of the shipping blockade and invasion of Naboo. Rune shares the monstrous green looks of Nute, and, like their leader Darth Sidious, both can appear as holograms while commanding droid forces to carry out their evil plans.

8

*"I will not condone a course of action
that will lead us to war."*

Queen Amidala, the young, recently elected leader of the planet Naboo, is no ordinary ruler. She has a regal beauty and presence that inspires awe and devotion among her subjects. She is a sight to behold, as she moves with elegance and grace, constantly attended by an entourage of advisors and handmaidens. Her royal gowns are spectacular, each one a glorious masterpiece.

But there's much more to Queen Amidala than beauty and wonderful outfits. Her loveliness is matched only by her compassion for the population of Naboo. There's no doubt she has the strength, wisdom, and courage of a great ruler.

This is a proud and determined queen who will not be crossed. She will stop at nothing to keep Naboo safe from the clutches of the invading Trade Federation. Queen Amidala truly embraces the spirit of the people of the lush green planet Naboo.

JAR JAR

"Monstair's back!"

This happy-go-lucky, amphibian creature has a charm all his own. He talks ten-to-the-dozen in his own peculiar slang. You just can't help liking Jar Jar, even if he is a rather clumsy individual. He comes from a race of beings called Gungans who live in the vast underwater city of Otoh Gunga on the green planet Naboo. Due to an unfortunate accident in the past, Jar Jar has been banished from his city. Still, this doesn't stop him from being kind, helpful, and honest at all times.

Jar Jar is also very knowledgeable about his native land and can reveal deeper qualities that perhaps he isn't fully aware of himself.

And while he often stumbles into danger, this sometimes works to his advantage. To his own surprise, Jar Jar can somehow manage to get himself out of the worst possible situations!

Underwater Menace!

The waters of Naboo conceal the amazing submerged bubble city of Otoh Gunga, home to the fascinating Gungans and ruled by the colourful Boss Nass.

On their perilous submarine journey from Otoh Gunga to the core of the planet, Qui-Gon, Obi-Wan and Jar Jar narrowly escape the clutches of several terrors of the deep - the opee sea killer...the sando aqua monster...and the dreaded colo claw fish!

STAR WARS
EPISODE I
The Phantom Menace

A long time ago in a galaxy far, far away ...

Turmoil has engulfed the Galactic Republic. The taxation of trade routes to outlying star systems is in dispute. Hoping to resolve the matter with a blockade of deadly battleships, the greedy Trade Federation has stopped all shipping to the small planet of Naboo.

While the Congress of the Republic endlessly debates this alarming chain of events, the Supreme Chancellor has secretly dispatched two Jedi Knights, the guardians of peace and justice in the galaxy, to settle the conflict ...

A Republic space cruiser raced towards the beautiful green planet of Naboo, which was surrounded by hundreds of Trade Federation battleships. The little craft slowed and manoeuvred close to one of the battleships.

The cruiser captain looked to her viewscreen, where Nute Gunray, a Nemoidian trade viceroy on the battleship's bridge, awaited the ship's arrival.

"With all due respect for the Trade Federation, the Ambassadors for the Supreme Chancellor wish to board immediately," she said.

"Yes, of course," came Nute's reply. "As you know, our blockade is perfectly legal."

The cruiser docked in the enormous main bay of the battleship and two darkly robed figures emerged and were greeted by protocol droid TC-14.

"A Republic cruiser," murmured a watching worker droid. "That's trouble, don't you think?"

"I'm not made to think," said his companion shortly.

The robed figures were left to wait in a conference room. They were Jedi: the tall, striking Qui-Gon Jinn and his young apprentice Obi-Wan Kenobi.

"I have a bad feeling about this," said Obi-Wan.

"Don't centre on your anxiety," replied his Master. "Keep your concentration here and now, where it belongs."

On the bridge of the battleship, Nute Gunray and Daultay Dofine were stunned to discover their visitors were Jedi.

"We're done for!" declared Dofine.

"Stay calm!" said Nute summoning up the hologram of their mysterious leader, a Sith Lord called Darth Sidious!

The Nemoidian grew more and more nervous.

"This turn of events is unfortunate, Viceroy," Darth Sidious said slowly. "Begin landing your troops!"

"And the two Jedi?"

"Kill them immediately."

A gun turret on the battleship swung round and blasted the waiting Republic ship. In the conference room Qui-Gon and Obi-Wan felt the disturbance, leapt up and drew their lightsabres. A faint hissing noise came and the room filled with a deadly green cloud.

"Gas!" cried Qui-Gon, and the two Jedi drew breath quickly and held it.

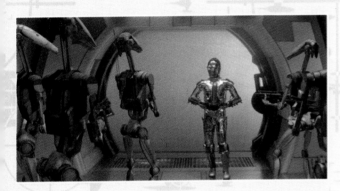

Battle droids outside cocked their weapons as one of their number opened the door cautiously. Two Jedi lightsabre beams flashed and the droids were quickly cut down, as Qui-Gon and Obi-Wan fought their way to the bridge.

Seated on the bridge Nute and his

comrade, Rune, were panicking. Qui-Gon's lightsabre appeared and he

began cutting through the door. Quickly Nute ordered the three thick blast doors to be closed, but still the Jedi came.

Suddenly a bunch of ugly droidekas appeared. Transforming from wheel form into battle configuration, they began blasting away with their own laserguns.

"They have shield generators!" exclaimed Obi-Wan.

"Let's go!" said Qui-Gon.

The two Jedi disappeared up a ventilation shaft which led them to a giant hangar bay, where thousands of battle droids were loading onto landing-craft — an invasion army!

"We've got to warn the Naboo and contact Chancellor Valorum," said Qui-Gon. "Let's split up. Stow aboard separate ships and meet down on the planet."

Meanwhile, on the battleship's bridge, the sly Nute was speaking on his viewscreen to Queen Amidala on Naboo. She sat, elaborately robed, surrounded by her governing council and handmaidens, Eirtaé, Yané, Rabé, Sabé and Saché.

"Your trade boycott of our planet has ended," declared the Queen. "I'm aware the Chancellor's Ambassadors are with you now, and that you have been commanded to reach a settlement."

"I know nothing about any ambassadors ... you must be mistaken," said Nute.

"Beware, Viceroy," warned the Queen. "The Trade Federation is going too far this time!" And, with that, she faded away.

The Queen then stood before a hologram of her ally, the kindly Senator Palpatine, to make a report. But his hologram spluttered and disappeared. The Trade Federation were jamming the transmission!

"A communications disruption can mean only one thing — invasion!" Governor Bibble warned the Queen. "We must prepare to defend ourselves!"

Darkness fell on Naboo and Trade Federation landing-craft descended in an eerie swamp. Obi-Wan's head emerged from the watery mud of

a shallow lake and he observed what was happening. He took several deep breaths, then submerged again.

A large droid force moved out of the swamp and onto a grassy plain. A small hologram of Nute and Rune stood on the tank of commander OOM-9 and supervised his handling of the invasion.

Qui-Gon had hitched an unseen ride with his enemies. Now he was running through the strange landscape, glancing back at the monstrous troop transports emerging from the mist. An odd, frog-like Gungan, Jar Jar Binks, was squatting down, holding a clam he had retrieved from the swamp. The shell popped open and Jar Jar's great tongue snapped out. He swallowed the clam in one gulp.

One of the huge MTT transports was bearing down upon him. Jar Jar stood transfixed. Then he grabbed on to Qui-Gon as he raced past. "Hep me, hep me!"

Qui-Gon caught him and pulled him down to safety in the mud.

"Oyi! I luv you!" cried Jar Jar, kissing the surprised Jedi. "Mesa you humbule servant!"

Obi-Wan suddenly burst out of the mist — chased by two battle droids on STAP vehicles. Qui-Gon pushed Jar Jar back into the mud. The STAPs fired laser bolts at Obi-Wan, but Qui-Gon deflected them back and blew up the STAPs!

Obi-Wan joined them and the grateful Jar Jar offered to take the Jedi to the safety of his underground city, Otoh Gunga, even though he'd been banished from the place for being clumsy.

The three ran to a murky lake, where Jar Jar said, "Wesa goen underwater, okeyday?"

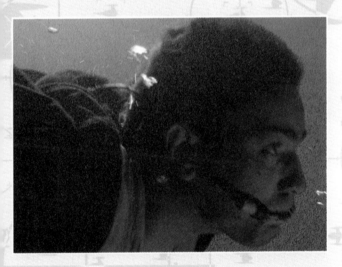

From their utility belts, Qui-Gon and Obi-Wan pulled out small capsules which turned into breathing-masks. Jar Jar did a double somersault into the water, and the Jedi followed.

They swam towards the distant glow of an underwater city made of large bubbles. The Jedi followed Jar Jar through a bubble-membrane which sealed behind them.

The Gungan leader was Boss Nass. His boardroom had bubble walls with small, lighted fish swimming around.

The room was filled with Gungan officials. Qui-Gon and Obi-Wan faced Boss Nass and explained what was happening.

"The droid army is about to attack the Naboo," said Qui-Gon. "We must warn them."

At first, Boss Nass was reluctant to help, but he agreed to give the Jedi a bongo for transport.

Qui-Gon noticed that Jar Jar was now in chains. "What is to become of him?" he asked.

"Pounded unto death," was the grim reply from Boss Nass.

"We need a navigator to take us through the core of the planet," said Qui-Gon. "I have saved Jar Jar's life — he owes me a life debt."

"Then begone wit him, outlander," said Boss Nass.

The promised bongo turned out to be a peculiar little submarine! In it, the Jedi and Jar Jar left Otoh Gunga and headed for the core of the planet. Jar Jar was of little use as a navigator, so Qui-Gon let the Force guide them.

A loud, sudden crash came, and the submarine lurched to one side.

An enormous, luminous opee sea killer had hooked them with its long, gooey tongue.

"Full speed ahead," said Qui-Gon.

The little craft was drawn into the creature's mouth.

Obi-Wan was a skilful pilot and the tiny sub broke free from the monster's jaws as a larger monster caught the opee in its teeth.

"Wesa free!" yelled Jar Jar.

"There's always a bigger fish," said Qui-Gon.

Soon there was more trouble ahead for the submariners. Sparks began flying, water leaked into the cabin and the drive lost power.

"Stay calm," Qui-Gon told Jar Jar, who was panicking.

The lights flickered back on, revealing an ugly colo claw fish directly in front of them.

"Monstair's back!" yelled Jar Jar. "Wesa in trouble?"

"Relax," said Qui-Gon, putting his hand on Jar Jar's shoulder

The creature reared back, then, leapt after the submarine and into the waiting jaws of the sando aqua monster.

"Wesa dead yet?" asked Jar Jar as he spotted the giant aqua monster. His eyes bulged at the sight and he fainted.

The submarine narrowly avoided the deadly teeth of the aqua monster, but the colo claw fish wasn't so lucky.

The little craft propelled upwards and bobbed to the surface in Theed estuary. The current began pulling the craft back into a fast-moving river straight towards a huge waterfall.

"Wesa die'n here, hey!" shouted Jar Jar.

But Qui-Gon came to the rescue. He shot out a thin cable, which wrapped around a railing on the shore just in time.

The submarine hung precariously over the waterfall's edge.

The Jedi clambered out and pulled themselves along the cable. The nervous Jar Jar had no choice but to follow them.

"Drop your weapons!" demanded a battle droid from the shore.

Qui-Gon responded by igniting his lightsabre and cutting the droid down in its tracks. A stray laser bolt hit the cable that held the bongo, and the Gungan submarine crashed down the waterfall.

"Whoa!" exclaimed Jar Jar, looking at all the mess.

Queen Amidala was in deep trouble. She had watched helplessly from a palace window as long columns of the battle droids moved down the road into Theed, the capital of Naboo. Now she, Governor Bibble, and five of her handmaidens were surrounded in the throne room by Nute, Rune and twenty droids. Captain Panaka and four Naboo guards were also held at blasterpoint.

"How will you explain this invasion to the Senate?" demanded Bibble.

"The Naboo and the Trade Federation will forge a treaty that will legitimise our occupation here," said Nute.

"I will not co-operate," said the Queen.

"Now, now, Your Highness! Your people's suffering will persuade you to see our point!"

The Queen and her entourage were led away through the plaza, filled with tanks and battle droids.

The Jedi and Jar Jar were making their way to the palace. Seeing the Queen, they jumped down from a balcony, surprising the group.

"We are the Ambassadors for the Supreme Chancellor," announced Qui-Gon to the astonished Queen.

"Your Highness, I suggest you come to Coruscant with us," said Qui-Gon. "They will kill you if you stay. There is no logic in the Trade Federation's move here."

The Queen agreed to go and plead her case before the Senate on Coruscant, leaving Bibble behind to do what he could. She and Captain Panaka,

took Qui-Gon, Obi-Wan, Jar Jar, two guards and three handmaidens — Padmé, Eirtaé and Rabé — to the main hangar, where the sleek, Royal Starship was docked.

Moving quickly, the Jedi dispatched the droid guards as alarms sounded.

"We need to free those pilots," said Captain Panaka, pointing to a group held under guard by droids. "I'll take care of that," Obi-Wan replied moving quietly away.

Obi-Wan managed to free the pilots while Qui-Gon dispatched the droids. Some of the pilots joined him on board the Queen's Royal Starship. As it took off, more droids rushed into the hangar, firing at it.

While pilot Ric Olié navigated towards the giant battleship, Obi-Wan took Jar Jar to the hold to keep him out of trouble.

"Ello, boyos," said the Gungan to a row of R-2 astromech droids.

The Queen's ship headed closer to the massive Trade Federation battleships. There were explosions all around and suddenly an alarm sounded in the cockpit!

"The shield generator's been hit," said Ric. "Hopefully the repair droids can fix it!"

In the hold, the droids were activated. They rushed to an air lock. A little blue droid screeched as it passed Jar Jar and was ejected to the exterior of the ship. The ship raced past

the massive Trade Federation battleship, which blasted two droids away, then another. Luckily the lone blue droid managed to carry out the repair work in time.

"Power's back! The little droid did it," cried Ric. "Deflector shields up, at maximum."

Now, safe from enemy fire, the ship raced away. But there was a problem: the hyperdrive was leaking and there was not enough power to take them to far-off Coruscant.

"We'll have to land for repairs,"

announced Qui-Gon, studying a chart on the monitor.

"Here, Master — Tatooine," pointed out Obi-Wan. "It's small ... out of the way. The Trade Federation has no presence there."

Panaka thought the planet of Tatooine was hardly the place to take Queen Amidala, as it was controlled by gangsters called the Hutts. But there was little alternative and he conceded to the Jedi's plan.

Captain Panaka turned his attention to the little droid which had saved them.

"What is its number?" asked the Queen.

The droid beeped. Captain Panaka scraped dirt off its side and read: "R2-D2, Your Highness."

"Thank you, Artoo-Detoo," smiled the Queen. She turned to Padmé.

"Clean this droid up the best

you can."

Presently a large yellow planet loomed directly ahead. The ship landed in a desert area on the outskirts of a spaceport in a swirl of dust.

Obi-Wan hoisted the hyperdrive out of a floor panel. "It's gone. We'll need a new one."

Qui-Gon moved closer to him. "Don't let anyone send transmissions. Be wary — I sense a disturbance in the Force."

"I feel it also, Master," said Obi-Wan.

Leaving Obi-Wan to watch the ship and Queen, Qui-Gon, the astromech R2-D2, and Jar Jar began to trek towards Mos Espa, a spaceport. But a moment later Captain Panaka and Padmé ran out of the ship.

"Her Highness commands you to take her handmaiden with you," said Captain Panaka.

"I don't have time to argue, but this

is not a good idea," replied Qui-Gon. He looked sternly at Padmé. "Stay close to me."

Back in the conference room on the Trade Federation battleship, Nute and Rune conferred with a hologram of Darth Sidious.

"Has the Queen signed the treaty?" demanded Darth Sidious.

"She has disappeared, My Lord," said Nute. "One Naboo cruiser got past the blockade."

A second Sith Lord appeared behind Darth Sidious, who said: "Viceroy, this is my apprentice, Lord Maul. He will find your lost ship ..."

Continued on page 24

19

Anakin Skywalker

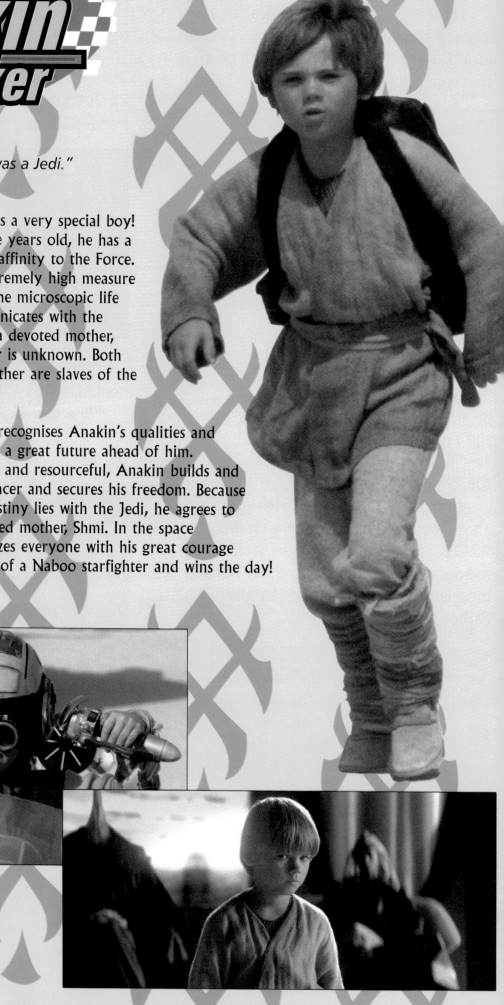

"I had a dream I was a Jedi."

Anakin Skywalker is a very special boy! Although only nine years old, he has a remarkably strong affinity to the Force. He possesses an extremely high measure of midi-chlorians, the microscopic life form which communicates with the Force. Anakin has a devoted mother, Shmi, but his father is unknown. Both Anakin and his mother are slaves of the junk dealer, Watto.

Qui-Gon instantly recognises Anakin's qualities and believes that he has a great future ahead of him. Clever, quick-witted and resourceful, Anakin builds and races his own Podracer and secures his freedom. Because Anakin feels his destiny lies with the Jedi, he agrees to leave his dearly loved mother, Shmi. In the space battle, Anakin amazes everyone with his great courage as he takes control of a Naboo starfighter and wins the day!

DARTH MAUL

The very sight of Darth Maul could strike fear into the bravest soul. A Sith Lord and loyal apprentice to Darth Sidious, his character is shrouded in mystery and his presence is ominous and brooding. Terrifying yellow eyes burn out from his horned, tattooed visage. This fearsome individual makes an athletic opponent who proves more than a match for Qui-Gon — and almost for Obi-Wan.

Soaked with the evil of the dark side, Maul's ferocity is lethal when unleashed. With his double-bladed lightsabre, Maul can lay waste to multiple adversaries with effortless ease and fluid grace. The Sith Lords' patience makes them even more dangerous — you just never know whether they are genuinely defeated or simply waiting to strike!

C-3PO

"I beg your pardon ... what do you mean I'm naked?"

It's amazing how some droids start out from the most humble and unexpected places. Take C-3PO for example. Built on the Outer Rim World of Tatooine and originally intended as a household servant, he is so far only partly assembled. He looks very strange, with a mass of wires and circuitry weaving in and out of a humanoid figure.

C-3PO is, in fact, an unfinished and unrefined human-cyborg relations droid. Though he has speech capability, he is not yet fully aware of his potential. As he develops, his status and duties will become clear. For C-3PO, the adventure is just beginning.

R2-D2

"Beep, beep ... whirr!"

You can depend on R2-D2! Exceptionally brave and resourceful, he stands out among the many astromech droids to be found on board Queen Amidala's spacecraft. His cylindrical body and domed head are covered with sensors and instruments. He stands upright on two legs and uses a third appendage when additional stability, or movement, is needed.

Faced with a bombardment of enemy fire, Artoo manages to save the Queen's ship from disaster. This feat of courage is just one example of his loyal service and fearless bravery. However dangerous the situation or deadly the enemy, this dedicated droid is sure to come through with flying colours.

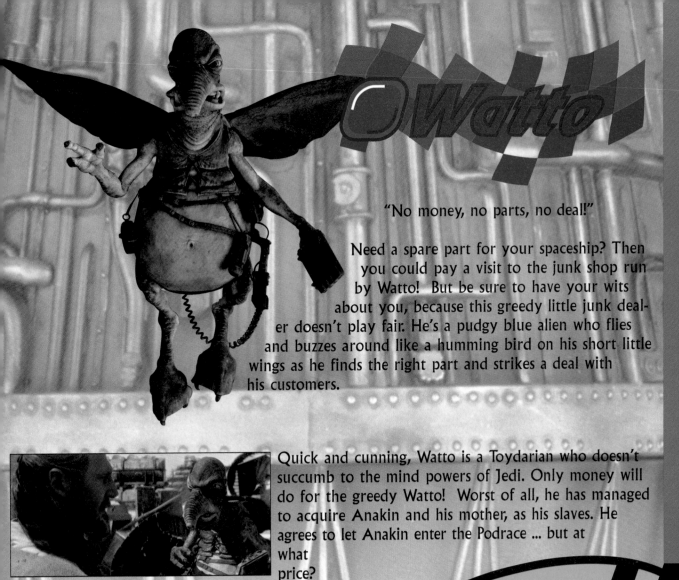

Watto

"No money, no parts, no deal!"

Need a spare part for your spaceship? Then you could pay a visit to the junk shop run by Watto! But be sure to have your wits about you, because this greedy little junk dealer doesn't play fair. He's a pudgy blue alien who flies and buzzes around like a humming bird on his short little wings as he finds the right part and strikes a deal with his customers.

Quick and cunning, Watto is a Toydarian who doesn't succumb to the mind powers of Jedi. Only money will do for the greedy Watto! Worst of all, he has managed to acquire Anakin and his mother, as his slaves. He agrees to let Anakin enter the Podrace ... but at what price?

SEBULBA

"You won't walk away from this one, slave scum!"

Sebulba may be the favourite in the Boonta Eve Podrace, but he's hardly a handsome hunk! This spider-like creature has plenty of dirty tricks up his sleeves and he'll stop at nothing in his efforts to win the day in his orange racer.

He's sore at Anakin before the race even begins. In the Mos Espa market, the boy stood up to him bravely in defence of clumsy Jar Jar, who accidentally flirted a dead frog into Sebulba's soup!

The Phantom Menace

Anakin and the Podrace

Qui-Gon and the group were soon in Mos Espa, which was bustling with dangerous-looking citizens of all types. They came to a little plaza surrounded by junk dealers and found a small shop with a pile of scrap stacked up behind it. Inside, the proprietor, a pudgy blue alien named Watto flew about like a humming bird.

"I need parts for a J-Type 327 Nubian," Qui-Gon told him.

"Ah, yes, we have lots." Watto raised his voice. "Boy, get in here!"

A dishevelled boy of about nine ran in from the junk yard. He was dirty and dressed in rags. He flinched as Watto scolded him.

"What took you so long?"

"I was cleaning the bin."

Watto took Qui-Gon and Artoo into the yard, leaving the boy with Padmé and Jar Jar.

"Are you an angel?" the boy asked Padmé. "I've heard the deep space pilots talk about them. They are the most beautiful creatures in the universe."

Padmé didn't know what to say.

"I'm a pilot," continued the boy. "Some day I'm going to fly away from this place." He continued telling her about his life.

To her horror, Padmé discovered that Watto had won the child and his mother in a bet. "You're a slave?" she asked.

"I am a person!" he corrected her defiantly. "My name is Anakin."

In the yard, Watto found the T-14 hyperdrive generator. Qui-Gon offered to pay in Republic credits, but Watto scoffed at the idea.

"I don't have anything else," said Qui-Gon, raising his hand and using his mind power. "But credits will do fine."

"No they won't!" came the reply.

"I'm a Toydarian. Mind tricks don't work on me —only money! Think you're some kind of Jedi waving your hand around like that?"

Qui-Gon hurried back into the shop with Artoo. "We're leaving," he said.

Padmé smiled at the boy. "I'm glad to have met you ... ah ..."

"Anakin," he replied. "Anakin Skywalker."

Qui-Gon, Padmé, Jar Jar and Artoo walked past a cafe full of rough-looking aliens. Jar Jar couldn't resist the sight of the gorgs hanging from a wire. He

whipped out his tongue and snapped one up into his mouth.

"Hey!" shouted the vendor.

In surprise, Jar Jar opened his mouth and the gorg, which was attached to the stand by a wire ricocheted out landing in the soup of an angry Dug, Sebulba. Sebulba grabbed Jar Jar and threw him to the ground.

"Why mesa always da one?" cried the hapless Gungan.

"Because you're afraid," came a calm voice. It was the boy, Anakin. "Careful, Sebulba, this one's very well connected, as in Hutt ..."

The Dug released Jar Jar and the others returned to find Jar Jar shaken. Anakin explained what had happened.

"Fear attracts the fearful," Anakin told the Gungan. "Be less afraid."

They continued along the street and stopped at a fruit stall run by an old woman named Jira.

The wind picked up strongly, and Anakin warned the group about sandstorms on Tatooine. There was no time for them to get back to their ship, so instead Anakin took the group back to his quarters - a slave hovel.

His mother, Shmi, was surprised to have guests, but she welcomed them. Anakin proudly showed Padmé the protocol droid he was building. He pushed a switch and the partly-finished droid, still without a covering body, sat up.

"How do you do. I am See-Threepio, human cyborg relations," it said in a very polite voice. "How might I serve you?"

Artoo let out a flurry of beeps and whistles.

"I beg your pardon?" replied Threepio."What do you mean I'm naked? Oh, my goodness. How embarrassing!"

A call came in on the comlink from Obi-Wan back at the ship. There had been news from Naboo. Governor Bibble sent a message saying all food supplies had been cut off and that the death toll was catastrophic. He had pleaded for Queen Amidala to answer and agree to bow to the wishes of the Trade Federation.

"It sounds like bait to establish a connection trace," said Qui-Gon.

"What if the people are dying?" asked Obi-Wan.

"Either way, we're running out of time ..."

While a gigantic sandstorm engulfed the town, Qui-Gon, Anakin, Shmi, Jar Jar, and Padmé sat around a table having dinner. Jar Jar used his tongue to snatch some food from a bowl at the other end of the table. Qui-Gon frowned at him.

"Have you ever seen a Podrace?" asked Anakin.

"Very fast, very dangerous," said Qui-Gon, nodding.

"I'm the only human who can do it," Anakin boasted.

"You must have Jedi reflexes if you race Pods."

"You're a Jedi Knight, aren't you? I saw your lightsabre," continued Anakin. "I had a dream that I was a Jedi. I came back here and freed all the slaves. Have you come to free us?"

Qui-Gon saw that there was no fooling the boy. He explained that they were on the way to Coruscant on an important mission, but that they were stranded on Tatooine until they could get the vital spare parts from Watto.

Anakin had a solution, but one which worried his mother terribly.

"I've built a Podracer — the fastest ever!" he announced.

"There's a big race tomorrow on Boonta Eve, and the prize money would more than pay for the parts."

Shmi shook her head as Anakin tried to persuade her that he should race. Finally she agreed. "Annie's right, there is no other way. He can help you ... he was meant to help you."

Qui-Gon and Anakin returned to Watto's shop to strike a deal.

"I have ... acquired a Podracer — the fastest ever built," said Qui-Gon.

The greedy Watto agreed to pay the entry fee for the forthcoming race, and to let his young slave pilot the Podracer. If Anakin won, Watto would keep the winnings minus the cost of the desperately needed spare parts. But if he lost, then Qui-Gon would hand over his ship to Watto!

Qui-Gon returned to Anakin's home and contacted Obi-Wan, who was still on the ship in the desert.

"What if this plan fails, Master?" asked Obi-Wan over the comlink. "We could be stuck here for a long time."

"A ship without a power supply will not get us anywhere," replied Qui-Gon. "And there is something about this boy ..."

Shmi appeared, and Qui-Gon told her she should be proud of her son. "He has special powers. The Force is unusually strong with him, that is clear. Who was his father?"

"There was no father," said Shmi. "I

carried him ... I gave birth ... I can't explain what happened."

"Had he been born in the Republic, he would have become a Jedi, no doubt. But it's too late now — he's too old."

Anakin, Padmé, and Artoo worked on the Podracer, helped by Anakin's friend Kitster and some other kids. Jar Jar assisted too, poking about and making a nuisance of himself.

At nightfall, Anakin sat on the balcony, chatting about the stars to Qui-Gon, who tended to a cut the boy had received. Qui-Gon wiped a little blood onto a comlink chip and, after the boy had gone to bed, inserted it into the comlink and asked Obi-Wan to run a midi-chlorian count.

"The reading's off the chart ... over twenty thousand," reported Obi-Wan. "Even Master Yoda doesn't have a count that high! What does it mean?"

"I'm not sure," pondered Qui-Gon.

In the desert, a sinister Sith spacecraft landed, scattering a herd of banthas. The dark figure of Darth Maul strode out of the ship and studied the

landscape with his electro-binoculars. He picked out the lights of the cities in the distance, then sent six small, globe-shaped probe droids towards them.

It was the day of the big race! At the large main hangar in Mos Espa arena, a dozen or so Podracers were being made ready. Alien crews and pilots rushed about.

Qui-Gon was discussing his agreement with Watto, and was surprised to find that Watto was betting heavily on Sebulba to win.

"I'll take that bet," said Qui-Gon. "I'll wager my new Podracer against Anakin and his mother."

"No, one slave or nothing," said Watto. He pulled a small cube from his pocket and tossed it down. "Blue it's the boy, red his mother."

It was blue, thanks to a little help from the Force and Qui-Gon, who smiled at the result.

"You won't win the race," said Watto angrily. "So it makes

little difference."

Meanwhile one of Darth Maul's probe droids floated slowly down the main street. It looked into shops, searching for Qui-Gon, Obi-Wan, or the Queen.

Large viewing platforms dominated the landscape of the desert racetrack, and more than a hundred thousand spectators had gathered in a large amphitheatre. Vendors sold barbecued creature parts and a range of colourful drinks.

"Greetings!" called out a two-headed announcer. "We have perfect weather for the Boonta Classic, the most hazardous of all Podracer races!"

A line of Podracers emerged from the hangar. The pilots bowed before the slug-like Jabba the Hutt in his royal box.

Sebulba and Anakin waited alongside each other on the

The crowds roared as Jabba finished announcing the contestants. Sebulba gave a sinister grin. "You won't walk away from this one, slave scum!" he taunted Anakin.

The boy strapped himself into the tiny racer.

"All set, Annie?" smiled Qui-Gon. "Remember, concentrate on the moment. Feel. Don't think — trust your instincts. May the Force be with you!"

Anakin donned his helmet. The pilots flipped their switches and

starting-grid. Sebulba waved to his fans and a small band started playing. Kitster attached two giant engines to Anakin's cockpit with cables.

Shmi kissed her son, and Jar Jar patted him on the back, saying, "May da guds be kind, mesa palo."

Then Padmé came up and kissed him lightly on the cheek. "You carry all our hopes," she said.

powerful energy binders shot between the huge engines. The deafening roar of high-powered racers echoed throughout the arena.

Qui-Gon joined Padmé and Jar Jar on a viewing platform which rose into the air.

"You Jedi are too reckless," said Padmé.

"The Queen trusts my judgement, young handmaiden. You

28

should, too," replied Qui-Gon.

"You assume too much," said Padmé.

The earth-pounding roar of the engines was deafening. Jabba the Hutt gave the go- ahead for the race to start. A great green light flashed. The race had begun!

The Podracers shot forward with a high-pitched scream. Anakin's engine coughed, then spluttered. Other Podracers swerved round him and disappeared down the track as Anakin struggled to re-start. Finally his engines burst to life again.

"There goes Skywalker," cried the announcer. "He'll be hard pressed to catch up!"

The Podracers flew across the desert. Sebulba rounded the first bend, side by side with Mawhonic. Sebulba drove his Podracer into his rival, forcing him to crash into a wall of rock in a terrible display of fire and smoke.

Meanwhile Anakin was overtaking the stragglers. One driver, Gasgano, kept trying to block him. Anakin backed off, then gunned it as Gasgano went over the cliff. Anakin sailed over Gasgano and sped on through a canyon. Four Tusken Raiders above took pot-shots at the Podracers. One shot ricocheted off Anakin's Podracer.

The crowd was watching the progress of the race on small, hand-held viewing screens. Jar Jar looked over the shoulder of a peculiar alien called Fanta, who promptly moved the screen out of Jar Jar's view.

Now Sebulba was being challenged by another racer. Sebulba let him pull alongside, then opened a side vent to allow his exhaust to cut through his

rival's engine. The Podracer blew up, and Sebulba veered away.

Sebulba entered the arena, closely followed by all the remaining racers. Qui-Gon, Padmé, Shmi, and Jar Jar shouted with joy as Anakin passed by. It was the second lap, and he was with the pack as they passed the main arena.

"Skywalker is moving up. He's in sixth place," said the announcer.

Ody Mandrell pulled up in the pits and droids began work on his engine. But one of the pit droids stood too close to the rear and was sucked in. The engine wheezed, then exploded!

Terter was closing in on the leader. Sebulba broke off a small piece of his racer and sent it into Terter's engine. Terter veered into Anakin, unhooking one of the main straps linking Anakin's engines to his cockpit.

Anakin struggled to keep control. The Pod swung near the broken strap,

and Anakin was able to grab it and hook it back onto the cockpit.

Sebulba cut the engine of another competitor with his side exhaust, and sent it crashing in a cloud of dust. Anakin went into the cloud. He hit part of an engine, but skilfully managed to regain control.

"At the start of the third and final lap, Sebulba is in the lead, closely followed by Skywalker!" boomed the announcer.

At last Anakin had caught up with Sebulba! They raced neck and neck

over the rough terrain. Sebulba tried his sly exhaust trick. Anakin avoided damage but was forced onto the service ramp. Then, on a tight bend, he dived to the inside and took the lead!

The furious Sebulba stayed on Anakin's tail, pressing him hard. All was well until one of Anakin's engines began to break loose. The boy switched to an auxiliary system but, in doing so, let Sebulba pass him.

Anakin tried repeatedly to get around Sebulba, who blocked his every move. Finally the boy faked a move to the inside — his favoured strategy — then switched to the outside. It worked! The two Podracers raced side by side down the final stretch of the track.

Sebulba crashed into Anakin over and over again. The boy struggled to maintain control when the steering rods of the two Podracers hooked together. Sebulba grinned wickedly.

As the pair approached the finishing-line, Anakin tried to pull away, but the strain snapped his steering-arm and sent his Podracer out of control. The release of tension sent Sebulba smashing into an ancient statue. One of his engines exploded, then the other. He slid to a smoking stop.

Anakin regained control and flew through the explosion. The crowds cheered. Padmé and Jar Jar jumped for joy. Artoo and Kitster whistled hysterically. Qui-Gon and Shmi smiled with satisfaction as the young racer crossed the line.

"It's Skywalker," yelled the announcer. "The crowd is going nuts!"

Anakin was a hero. The spectators surged forward and carried him shoulder-high. But through the cheering and chanting, Darth Maul's searching probe drifted menacingly.

Qui-Gon went to collect his winnings from Watto, who was not at all keen to deliver. He poked his face against Qui-Gon's.

"Bring the parts to the main hangar," smiled Qui-Gon. "I'll come by your shop later so you can release the boy."

The probe droid watched the scene ... with great interest.

The main hangar was almost deserted as the Podracers departed. Inside, Jar Jar, Padmé, and Shmi hugged Anakin in turn. Now Qui-Gon had the vital ship parts in containers and he lost no time in harnessing them to huge eopies. Padmé and Qui-Gon climbed onto one of the creatures. Jar Jar climbed onto another, then slid hopelessly off the other side. Anakin and Shmi waved them all goodbye and watched them set off back to the ship.

The probe droid was watching, too. It observed them unloading their spoils at the ship in the desert, then it turned and sped away ...

Qui-Gon kept his promise and soon returned for Anakin.

"These are yours," he told the boy, giving him a handful of coins. "We sold the Podracer."

They entered Anakin's home and the delighted boy showed his mother all the money.

"And Anakin has been freed," said the Jedi.

Anakin and Shmi were stunned.

"Will you take him with you?" Shmi asked. "Is he to become a Jedi?"

Qui-Gon turned to the boy. "Nothing happens by accident. You are strong with the Force, but you may not be accepted by the Council."

"A Jedi!" exclaimed Anakin. "Mighty blasters, you mean I get to go with you in your starship and everything!?"

Qui-Gon kneeled to the boy's level and told him of the hard life that lay ahead.

"I want to go," said Anakin.

"Then pack your things. We haven't much time."

"Yippee!"

As he prepared to go, Anakin realised his mother would not be coming. Qui-Gon had not been able to free her, and the proceeds from selling the Podracer were not nearly enough to buy her freedom.

"It's time for you to let go of me," she said, drawing her son close. "Listen to your feelings, Annie. You know what's right."

"I'm going to miss you so much, Mom," said the boy tearfully.

"I love you, Annie ... now hurry."

Anakin threw his belongings into a small backpack. He said farewell to the still unfinished Threepio, and handed some coins to Kitster.

As he left to go, he ran back to his mother in the doorway and hugged her, saying, " I can't do it."

"No matter where you are, my love will be with you," she said. "Now be brave... and don't look back."

Qui-Gon and Anakin set off.

As they headed down the street, Qui-Gon suddenly drew his lightsabre and lunged forward at a lurking probe droid, slicing it, fizzling, in half.

"Probe droid," he mused. "Very unusual ... not like anything I've seen before. Come on."

The Jedi and his young companion made their way back across the desert. Qui-Gon was running as they neared the waiting ship, and Anakin found it hard to keep up with him.

"Wait, Master," he shouted.

Qui-Gon turned to answer, and spotted Darth Maul, on a speeder bike, bearing down on them.

He shouted for Anakin to drop, which he did — just as Darth Maul swept over him. The Sith Lord jumped from the bike and, even before he hit the ground, swung a lightsabre blow that Qui-Gon was barely able to block.

A bewildered Anakin picked himself up and watched the Sith and Jedi locked in fierce lightsabre battle.

"Annie, get to the ship," cried Qui-Gon. "Take off! Go!"

The boy ran quickly and found Captain Panaka and Padmé.

The battle continued, with the two galactic warriors jumping over one another in an incredible display of acrobatics. Shortly they heard the ship, now repaired, hovering just above the ground. Before Darth Maul knew what had happened, Qui-Gon was on the spacecraft's ramp.

Darth Maul jumped onto the ramp too but barely made it, with his heels hanging over the edge. As the craft rose skyward, Qui-Gon swung his lightsabre and knocked Darth Maul down onto the desert floor. The ramp closed and the ship rocketed away from Tatooine.

"Let's hope this hyperdrive works," said Qui-Gon.

Pilot Ric Olié pulled back the control — and the ship streaked off into hyperspace!

Continued on page 40

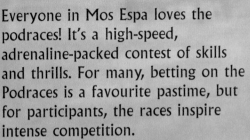

Everyone in Mos Espa loves the podraces! It's a high-speed, adrenaline-packed contest of skills and thrills. For many, betting on the Podraces is a favourite pastime, but for participants, the races inspire intense competition.

A Podracer is essentially a small cockpit pulled by two high-powered engines, and each one is usually heavily customised to match the demands of the individual pilot. Podracing requires quick reflexes and strong nerves. As a result, almost all Podracers are non-human.

Every Podrace is hazardous, but in some, such as the Boonta Eve Race at the Mos Espa Arena, presided over by Jabba the Hutt, the danger is extreme. The course winds its way through canyons and tunnels, and the Podracers are at risk of being hit by sniping pot-shots from Tusken Raiders. To the delight and excitement of the crowd, many Podracers routinely crash and burn, but fame and fortune awaits those who emerge victorious.

Sebulba ready to go.

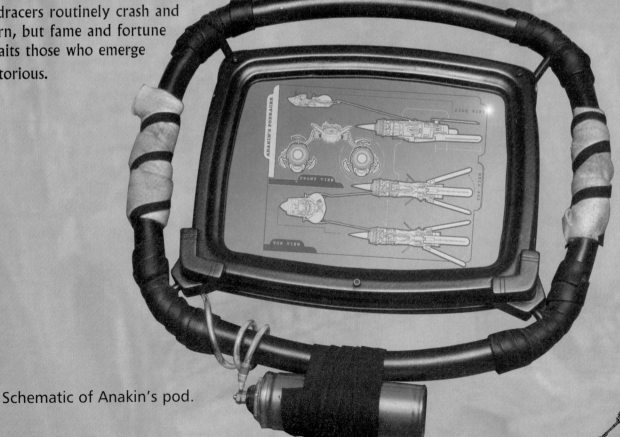

Schematic of Anakin's pod.

Anakin and Sebulba race.

The crowd looks on.

34

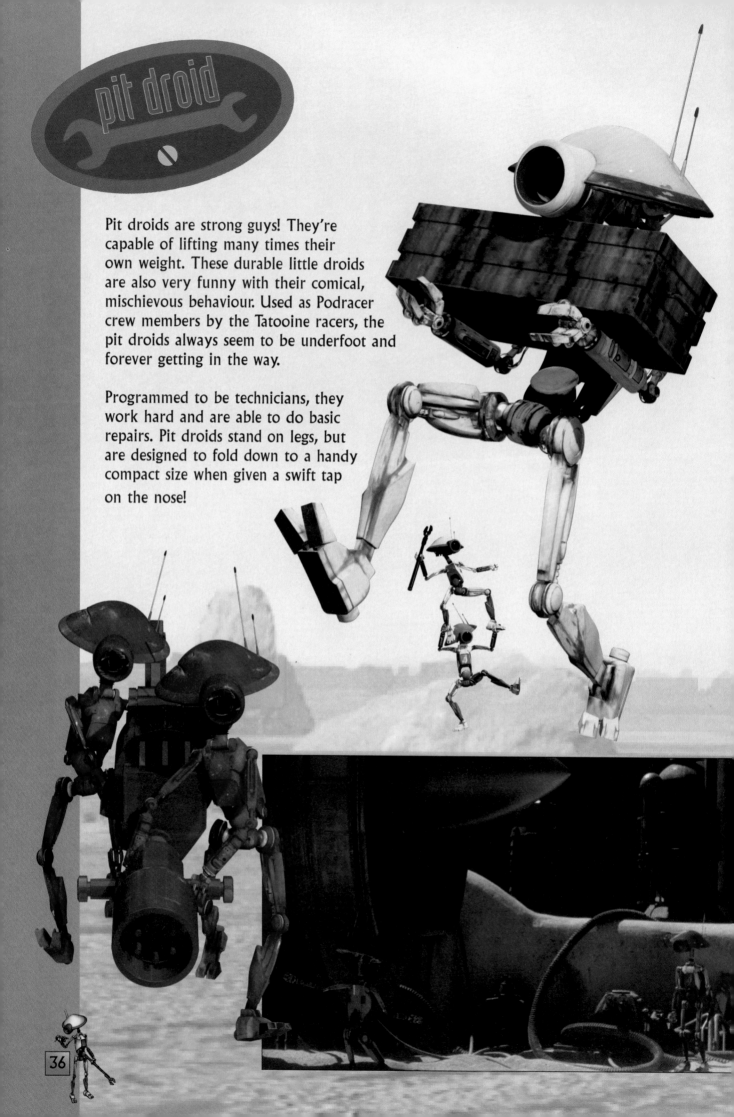

pit droid

Pit droids are strong guys! They're capable of lifting many times their own weight. These durable little droids are also very funny with their comical, mischievous behaviour. Used as Podracer crew members by the Tatooine racers, the pit droids always seem to be underfoot and forever getting in the way.

Programmed to be technicians, they work hard and are able to do basic repairs. Pit droids stand on legs, but are designed to fold down to a handy compact size when given a swift tap on the nose!

TOOLS OF EVIL

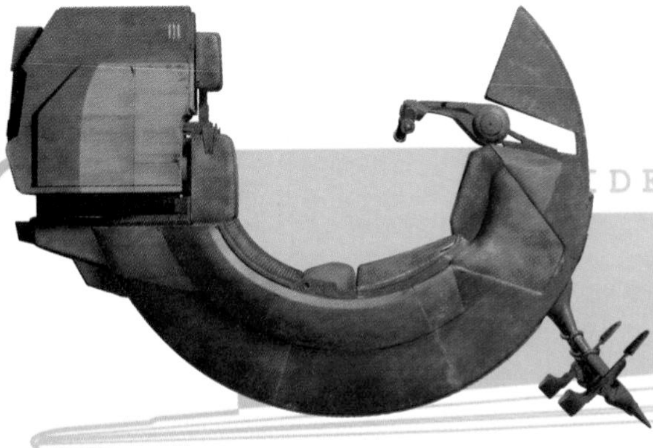

Sith Speeder bike

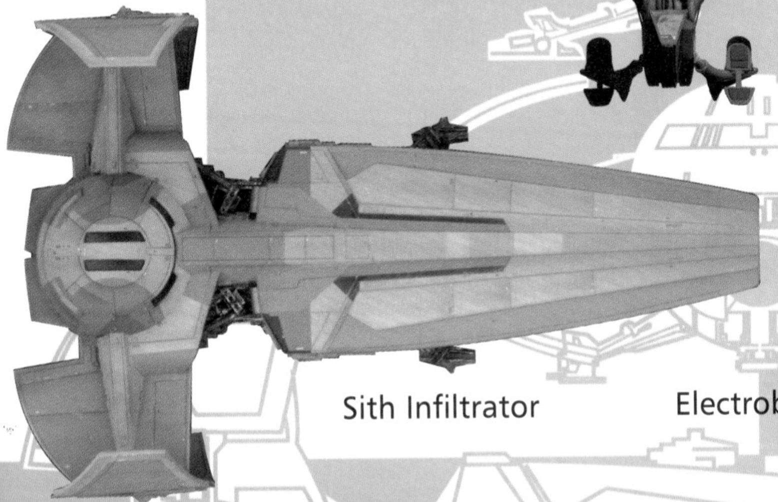

Sith Infiltrator

Electrobinoculars

BACK VIEW

Darth Maul has many weapons and items at his disposal and each one can be put to use in the apprehension of his prey.

As if the shattering combat skills aren't enough, he is backed up by a wealth of sophisticated hardware.

Amongst his arsenal are dark eye probe droids, these small black orbs have artificial intelligence and drift around, watching and listening.

Maul's personal transport is his Infiltrator, this incorporates the most advanced technology.

On the ground he takes to his speeder bike which glides along.

Finally there is the Sith Lord's unique lightsabre, the sabre has twin blades giving him twice the power.

Lightsabre

Dark Eye Probe Droid

JEDI COUNCIL

"You're referring to the prophecy of the one who will bring balance to the force … you believe it's this boy?" **Mace Windu**

On Coruscant, the capital of the Republic, the tall spires of a unique building stand out against the skyline. This is the Temple of the Jedi, and here in the Council Chambers the twelve wise Jedi agree to see young Anakin and test him with a view to permitting training.

Sitting centrally is the senior Jedi, Mace Windu, between Ki-Adi-Mundi and Yoda — the Jedi Master with the intriguing speech pattern.

Despite Qui-Gon's faith in Anakin, the Jedi members sense anger and fear in the boy. They conclude that he poses a future threat and forbid Qui-Gon to train him.

Even Obi-Wan agrees. "The boy is dangerous … they all sense it," he tells his Master. "Why can't you?"

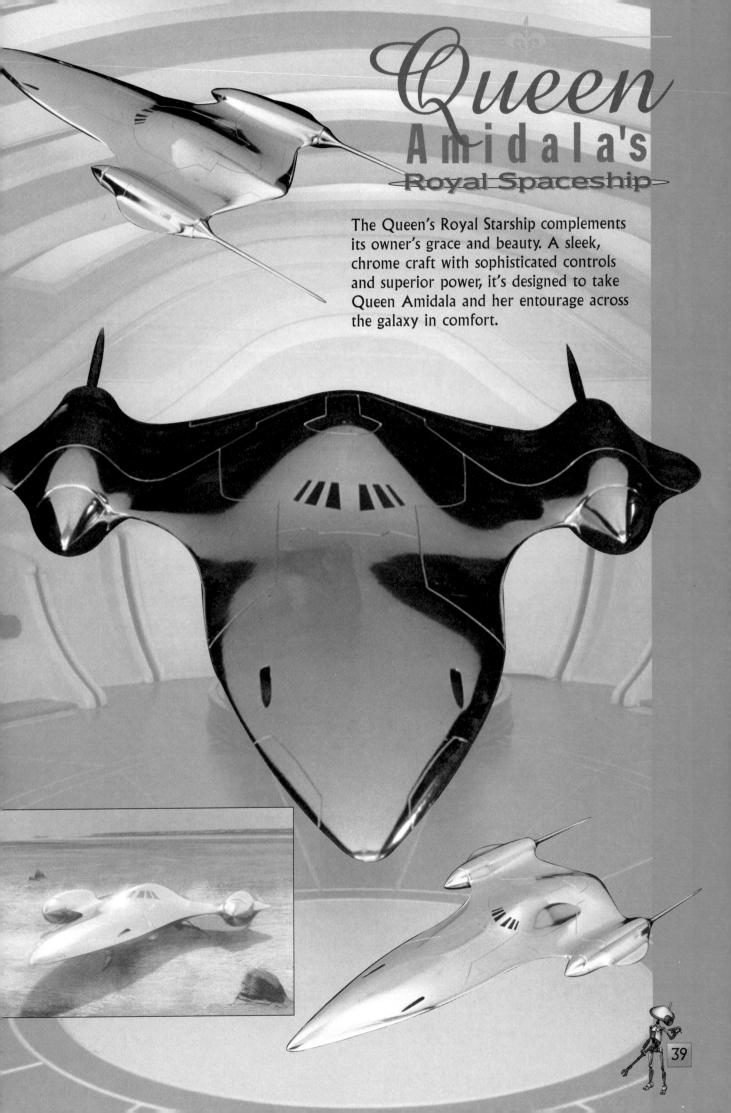

Queen
Amidala's
Royal Spaceship

The Queen's Royal Starship complements its owner's grace and beauty. A sleek, chrome craft with sophisticated controls and superior power, it's designed to take Queen Amidala and her entourage across the galaxy in comfort.

The Phantom Menace
A visit to Coruscant

The ship was cruising with its lights dimmed — most of the travellers were asleep. Padmé watched a recording of

Governor Bibble's plea. Jar Jar was stretched out on the floor, and Artoo rested peacefully.

Padmé sensed someone watching her. She found Anakin huddled in a corner, shivering and dejected, and she put her jacket round him.

"The Queen is worried," she explained to the boy sadly. "Her people are suffering ... dying. She must convince the Senate to intervene, or I'm not sure what will happen."

"I'm not sure what's going to happen to me," said Anakin. He gave her a carved wooden pendant. "I made this, so you'd remember me. It will bring you good fortune."

Padmé put it round her neck. "It's beautiful, but I don't need it to remember you, Annie. My caring for you will always remain."

She hugged him.

At last the ship reached Coruscant, capital of the Republic. The entire planet was one big city. Supreme Chancellor Valorum, Senator Palpatine, and several guards

waited on a landing platform as the Naboo spacecraft landed.

Qui-Gon, Obi-Wan, Jar Jar, and Anakin descended the ramp and bowed. Captain Panaka, two guards, and Queen Amidala came next, her handmaidens and more guards followed.

"It is a great gift to see you alive, Your Majesty," said Palpatine.

An air taxi was waiting. Qui-Gon, Obi-Wan, and Valorum watched as it took Palpatine, the Queen, Jar Jar, Anakin, and the three handmaidens to the Senator's quarters. There, Palpatine spoke seriously to the Queen: "The Senate is now full of greedy, squabbling delegates. I must be frank, Your Majesty, there is little chance the Senate will act on the invasion."

He went on to explain that Chancellor Valorum was involved with baseless accusations of corruption and had little real power.

It was necessary, he said, to push for the election of a stronger Supreme Chancellor. One who would enforce the laws and deliver justice.

Meanwhile Qui-Gon and Obi-Wan had gone to the Temple of the Jedi. They stood in the centre of a tall, stately room, before a semi-circle of twelve seated Jedi. A Senior Jedi named Mace Windu sat before them. To his left was Jedi Ki-Adi-Mundi, and to his right was Jedi Master Yoda.

Qui-Gon told them of the violent confrontation in the desert. "My only conclusion can be that it was a Sith Lord."

"Impossible!" declared Ki-Adi. "The Sith have been extinct for a millennium."

"The very Republic is threatened, if involved the Sith are," said Yoda.

"With this Naboo Queen you must stay, Qui-Gon. Protect her."

Qui-Gon reported to Yoda that he had encountered a vergence in the Force: Anakin, a boy with the highest concentration of midi-chlorians he had seen in a life form.

"You're referring to the prophecy of the one who will bring balance to the

Force?" asked Mace Windu.

"I request the boy be tested," said Qui-Gon.

The Jedi looked at one another, then nodded.

"Tested he will be," announced Yoda.

In the main rotunda of the Galactic Senate, thousands of Senators and their aides sat in the huge circular assembly area. Hundreds of aides and droids milled around. Valorum sat in a central, elevated position. Palpatine and Queen Amidala sat in the Naboo congressional box — a floating platform.

The Naboo box floated into the centre, and Palpatine addressed the assembly, telling of the tragedy that had befallen peaceful Naboo.

Then into the centre rushed another box, filled with Trade Federation barons. "This is outrageous! I object to the Senator's statements!" complained their leader, Lott Dod.

Valorum sent them back to their place, and the Queen rose to her feet.

"The Naboo system has been invaded by force," she said. "Invaded ... against all the laws of the Republic."

Lott Dod objected again, saying

there was no proof. He suggested a commission be sent to Naboo to discover the truth. The Congress of Malastare, in a third box, agreed.

The Queen was angry. "I was not elected to see my people die while you discuss this invasion in a committee. New leadership is needed. I move for a vote of no confidence in Chancellor Valorum's leadership!"

Her speech caused a great stir and a roar of approval and jeers. Someone seconded the motion. The assembly began to chant, "Vote now! Vote now!"

"You see, the tide is with us," Palpatine told the Queen. "They will elect a strong Chancellor, one who will not let our tragedy continue ..."

Anakin was undergoing tests at the Palace of the Jedi. Qui-Gon and

Obi-Wan waited on the balcony.

"The boy will not pass the Council's tests, Master," said Obi-Wan. "He is far too old."

"Anakin will become a Jedi, I promise you," replied Qui-Gon.

"Don't defy the Council, Master, not again," Obi-Wan implored him. "You could be sitting on the Council by now if you would just follow the code."

Inside, Anakin stood before the twelve Jedi, each had a viewscreen. A series of images flash across in rapid succession and Anakin had

to identify them. "A ship ... a cup ... a speeder..."

"Good, good, young one," said Yoda. "How feel you?"

"Cold, sir."

"Afraid, are you?"

"No, sir."

"Afraid to give up your life?" asked

Mace Windu.

"I don't think so."

"You thoughts dwell on your mother," observed Ki-Adi.

"I miss her."

"Afraid to lose her, I think," said Yoda.

"Fear is the path to the dark side. Fear leads to anger ... anger leads to hate ... hate leads to suffering."

The Queen and Jar Jar stood at a window in Palpatine's quarters, watching the sunset. Jar Jar saw how sad she looked.

"Mesa wonder why da guds invent pain?" he said. "Yousa tinken yousa

people ganna die?"

"I don't know."

"Gungans ganna get pasted too, eh? Gungans no die without a fight. Wesa got a grande army. Dat why you no like us, metinks."

Palpatine and Captain Panaka rushed in and bowed. They had good news.

"Your Highness, Senator Palpatine has been nominated to succeed Valorum," said Captain Panaka.

"If I am elected I will bring democracy back to the Republic," added Palpatine.

"I fear by the time you have control, there will be nothing left," replied the Queen. "I have decided to go back to Naboo. I will sign no treaty — my fate will be no different from that of our people."

The Jedi had made their decision

about Anakin's future.

"He will not be trained," Ki-Adi told Qui-Gon. "There is too much anger in him."

"He is the chosen one," countered Qui-Gon. "I will train him, then. I take Anakin as my Padawan learner!"

Yoda reminded him that he already had an apprentice, but Qui-Gon argued that Obi-Wan was ready to become a Knight.

Mace Windu was more concerned about the impending confrontation.

"Go with the Queen to Naboo and discover the identity of this dark warrior."

"I brought Anakin here. He must stay with me," insisted Qui-Gon.

"Train him not. Take him with you, but train him not!" said Yoda.

"May the Force be with you."

Qui-Gon, Obi-Wan, and Anakin waited on the Senate landing platform. Artoo whistled a happy tune as he leaned over the edge and watched the traffic ... went too far and toppled overboard! After a moment he reappeared, using his on-board jets to propel himself back onto the platform.

Anakin listened to the two Jedi talking.

"The boy is dangerous," said Obi-Wan. "They all sense it. Why can't you?"

When they had boarded the spacecraft, followed by Artoo, Anakin said, "Master Qui-Gon, sir, I do not wish to be a problem."

"You won't be, Annie. I'm not allowed to train you, so I want you to watch me and be mindful."

"Master, sir, what are midi-chlorians?" asked the boy.

Qui-Gon explained that they were a microscopic life form, residing within all living cells, which communicated with the Force. And that by learning to quieten your mind, you could hear them speaking to you.

"I don't understand," said Anakin.

"With time and training, Annie ... you will," said Qui-Gon.

Captain Panaka, Palpatine, troop guards, and officers entered the ship, followed by Queen Amidala, the handmaidens and, finally, Jar Jar.

The Trade Federation was aware of the Queen's movements. In the Naboo Throne Room, Nute and Rune stood before a hologram of the sinister Darth Sidious.

"The Queen is on her way to you. When she gets there, destroy her!" ordered the Sith Lord. "Is the planet secure?"

"Yes, my Lord," said Nute. "We are in complete control now."

"Good. I am sending Darth Maul to join you. He will deal with the Jedi ..."

The Queen's ship approached the lush green planet. Only one Trade Federation battlecruiser was in evidence.

"I have one battleship on my scope," said Ric Olié.

"A Droid Control Ship," said Obi-Wan.

They landed in the Gungan swamp. Jar Jar swam down into the Bubble City and was amazed to find the plaza empty. He returned to the ship to report his findings. "Dare-sa nobody dare! All gone. Sorry, no Gungas."

Obi-Wan suggested they had been wiped out, but Jar Jar disagreed. "Gungan hiden. When in trouble, go to sacred place."

The Group followed Jar Jar as he moved through the swamp.

He stopped and sniffed the air. "Dissen it." Then he made a strange chattering noise which brought, seemingly out of nowhere, Captain

Tarpals and six other Gungan troops riding kaadus.

"Binks! Noah gain!" cried the Captain.

"Ouch time for all-n youse."

The group was led through a clearing full of Gungan refugees to the ruins of a grand temple decorated with massive carved heads. Boss and several other Council Members walked out on top of a partly submerged head.

The Queen stepped forward. "I am Queen Amidala of the Naboo. I come in peace."

"Naboo biggen!" said Boss. "Yousa bringen da mackineeks. Yousa all die'n, mesa tink."

The Gungan troops lowered their power poles ominously.

"We wish to form an alliance," said the Queen.

But then Padmé stepped forward and announced, "Your Honour — I am Queen Amidala!" She pointed to the Queen. "This is my decoy ... my loyal bodyguard."

Anakin was stunned. Qui-Gon and Obi-Wan gave one another a knowing look.

"I am sorry for the deception. It has become necessary to protect myself," she continued. "Although we do not always agree, Your Honour, our two great societies have always lived in peace. The Trade Federation has destroyed all that we have worked so hard to build. I ask you to help us ... no, I beg you to help us!"

She dropped to her knees, and so did the rest of the group, including the two Jedi.

Boss Nass began to laugh. "Yousa no tinken yousa greater den da Gungans. Maybe wesa bein friends ..."

Nute, Rune and Darth Maul stood in the throne room before a hologram of Darth Sidious.

"We've already located their starship in the swamp," said Nute.

"It won't be long, my lord."

"This is an unexpected move for the Queen. It's too aggressive," growled Sidious. "Lord Maul, be mindful. Let them make the first move."

Amidala and the Jedi were discussing battle plans with the Gungan generals.

Boss Nass put his arm round Jar Jar. "Yousa doen grand. So, wesa maken yousa Bombad General."

"General!? Oh no!" cried Jar Jar.

His eyes rolled back, his tongue flopped out, and he fainted.

Four speeders pulled up. Panaka and a dozen guards piled out.

"Almost everyone's in camps. A few hundred police and guards have formed an underground movement," Panaka told the Queen. "I brought as many of the leaders as I could. The Trade Federation Army's much larger than we thought. This is a battle I do not think we can win."

But Queen Amidala had an answer. "The battle is to be a diversion. The Gungans must draw the droid army away from the cities. We can enter using the secret passages. Captain Panaka will make a diversion, so that we can enter the palace and capture the viceroy. Without him, the army will be lost and confused."

Nute, Rune, Darth Maul, and now OOM-9 were in the throne room again with a hologram of Darth Sidious.

"We are sending all available troops to meet this army of the Queen's

assembling near the swamp," said Nute. "It appears to be made up of primitives."

"I feel there is more to this, My Master," ventured Darth Maul. "The two Jedi may be using the Queen for their own purposes."

"The Jedi cannot become involved," replied Darth Sidious. "They can only protect the Queen. This will work to our advantage."

Continued on page 55.

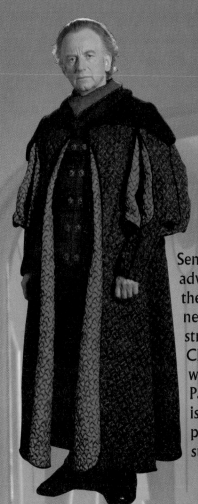

"I will bring peace back to the Republic."

Senator Palpatine acts as Queen Amidala's kindly ally, advising and helping her in times of trouble, such as during the shipping blockade. It is he who informs the Queen of the necessity to elect a new, stronger Supreme Chancellor in place of the weak Valorum. Senator Palpatine himself is nominated for the position, which he then succeeds in winning.

CAPTAIN PANAKA

"This is a battle I do not think we can win."

A dynamic and charismatic leader in the battle against the Trade Federation, Captain Panaka is a formidable commander of the Royal Naboo Security Forces and goes into action alongside Padmé.

DARTH SIDIOUS

"Wipe them out. All of them!"

Beware the calm, measured tones of Darth Sidious, for it is he who masterminds the demise of the Republic. The mysterious Sith Lord is seen only as a hologram — but that is more than enough to inspire a sense of dread. This robed, shadowy figure is the true power behind the greedy Trade Federation. As he manipulates events across the galaxy and dictates orders to Nemoidian trade viceroys Nute Gunray and Rune Haako, the true and terrible nature of his intentions and his frightening powers are revealed.

Darth Sidious has sinister designs against the peaceful planet Naboo, as well as its young Queen and the noble Jedi who protect her. It can't be said that anyone is actually close to this evil individual, with the possible exception of his dangerous apprentice, Darth Maul. As more becomes known about these two, the more the galaxy has to fear ...

The battle lines are drawn! On the grassy plains of Naboo, beneath bright sunshine and blue skies, a Gungan army, led by General Ceel, attempts to divert the Trade Federation droid forces away from the Theed Royal Palace. Past disagreements between the Gungans and the Naboo are forgotten. The Gungans have mastered all their resources: powerful energy balls, spear-throwing warriors mounted on Kaadu, and massive shield generators for additional protection from enemy artillery.

But is all this a match for the sophisticated weaponry, battalions of battle, and destroyer droids of their formidable opponent? The Trade Federation, co-ordinated by an orbiting battleship and the droid ground commander, OOM-9, has armoured attack tanks, flying STAPs, and large transporters. A deadly contrast to the comparatively primitive Gungans. Only time will tell!

Trade Federation landing craft. These are used to deploy the battle droids down on to the surface of a planet.
The craft can carry a vast number of troops and equipment.

49

The battle droid can quickly move around on a STAP.

The Trade Federation Tanks, or AATs, glide, over any terrain with menacing purpose.

Battle droids lining up after coming out of
the Trade Federation large transporters.

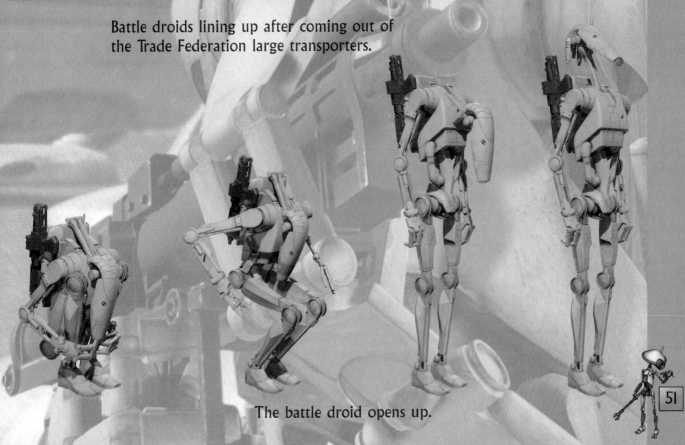

The battle droid opens up.

51

SPACE BATTLE

The Trade Federation must be defeated! The green planet Naboo must be freed to return to peace and prosperity under its newly elected young Queen Amidala. High above the planet, a desperate attempt is made to destroy the enemy's Droid Control Ship. Without their nerve centre, the Trade Federation droid army will be left immobilised and the tide of battle will surely turn in the Queen's favour.

But the odds are stacked heavily against the Naboo forces. Facing this most dangerous mission are the courageous pilots of Bravo Squadron, now liberated from captivity in Theed. Led by veteran pilot Ric Olié, the graceful Naboo starfighters go into battle against the scores of deadly Trade Federation droid fighters, plus the armour and turbolasers of the massive Droid Control Battleship itself.

Into this maelstrom of combat appears a single Naboo starfighter with young Anakin Skywalker at the controls. While the mission of Bravo Squadron is daunting, help towards victory may well come from a most unexpected quarter!

The Trade Federation presents a fearsome set of vehicles. The giant transports, the huge battleships, and the Droid Control Ship that proves to be the weak link, exploited by the most unlikely of pilots! In contrast to the graceful Naboo ships, Trade Federation droid starfighters have a repellent, crab-like appearance. The massive battleships and the Droid Control Ships have a sinister quality, while the MTT transporters resemble gigantic locomotives from the sky.

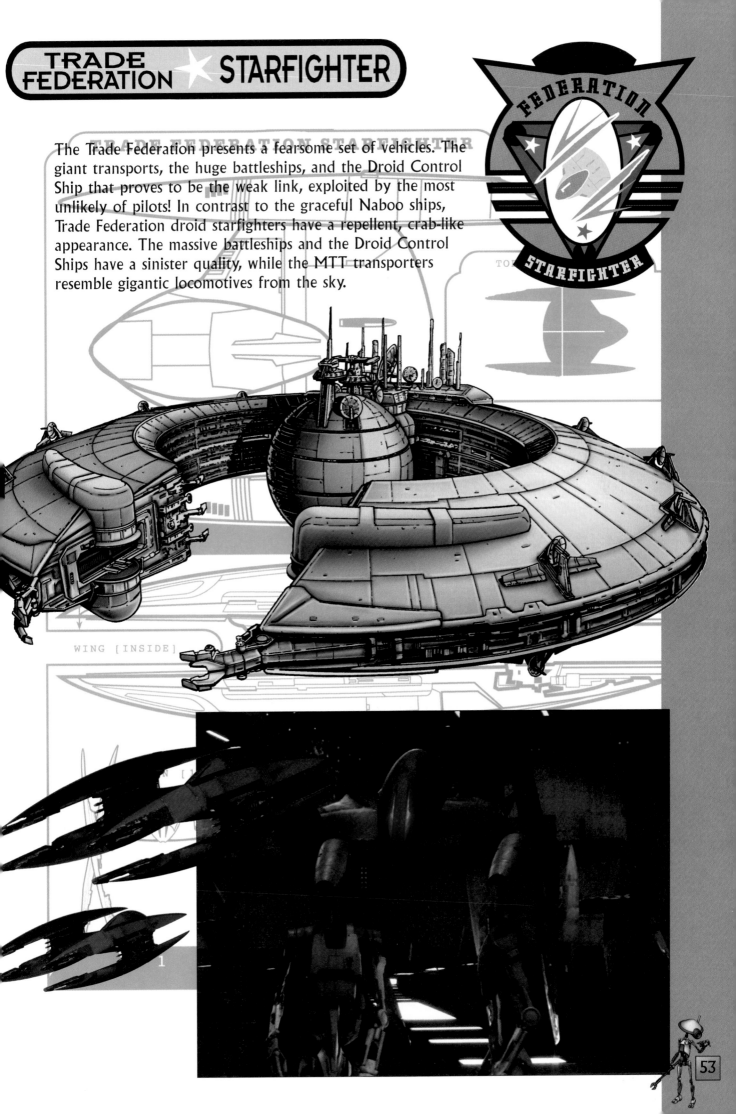

WING [INSIDE]

NABOO STARFIGHTER

The Naboo ships are sleek and fast, with chrome fronts and long, narrow back tails. Swift and agile in flight, they're designed for maximum manoeuvrability. The ideal craft for Bravo Squadron to take into battle.

The Phantom Menace
The battles for freedom

Everything appeared peaceful at the swamp lake — until a Gungan soldier astride a kaadu rose from the water, followed by several others. Jar Jar was riding high until his kaadu shook itself dry, dislodging the Gungan.

Soldiers on huge, lizard-like fambaas, with large shield generators mounted on their backs, emerged next. The Gungan army set out across the rolling grassy hills, its hundreds of warriors marching in long lines towards the horizon.

The Gungan General Ceel spotted Trade Federation tanks on the ridge ahead and ordered his army to stop.

"Energise the shields!" he commanded.

A red ray shot out of the fambaa mounted generator and blasted into a large dish on the back of a second fambaa before it spread like an umbrella over the assembled warriors.

The Trade Federation tanks fired on the Gungans. Their energy shield repelled the blasts and the Gungans cheered. Then they saw the doors of

the massive transports open, and ranks of battle droids deployed. OOM-9 gave the command, and thousands of battle droids moved forward.

The Gungans stood ready with their weapons, but the droids marched through the protective shield and started firing. The Gungans fought back with their power poles and small balls of energy flung with slingshots. They dumped large balls of energy into mortars and fired the energy-goo onto the droids, shorting them out.

Amidala, Qui-Gon, Obi-Wan, Anakin, Artoo, and a few members of the Security Forces, made their way stealthily to the entrance of the main hangar. The Queen signalled across the plaza to Captain Panaka and his assorted Naboo troops.

Droids milled around the tank-filled plaza. They fired on the rebels, and the Naboo soldiers fired back. The battle had begun!

The Queen and her troops rushed into the hangar as alarms sounded. Battle droids fired on the troops who

ran for cover. The Jedi deflected bolts back at the droids, destroying them.

Once inside, the Queen signalled to her pilots, "Get to your ships!"

The pilots and R-2 units rushed to the Naboo fighter craft. One of the pilots jumped into the fighter Anakin was hiding in.

"Better find a new hiding place, kid," he said. "I'm taking this ship."

A moment later the fighter rose out of the hangar. Battle droids fired as it fell into place behind five other departing fighters. From another stationary fighter, Artoo whistled to Anakin to come and hide.

Captain Panaka and his troops rushed into the hangar, overwhelming the few remaining battle droids and joining forces with the Queen's unit.

"My guess is the viceroy is in the throne room," said Padmé.

The group moved toward the exit, passing the fighter where Anakin was hiding.

"You stay there," said Qui-Gon noticing the boy. "Stay right where you are."

As they were about to leave, the threatening figure of Darth Maul appeared in the doorway. Qui-Gon and Obi-Wan moved forward. They removed their robes and ignited their lightsabres. Darth Maul did the same.

Both ends of his weapon lit up.

At the far end of the hangar, droidekas rolled in and transformed into their combat form. Artoo whistled, alerting Anakin to the droids advancing and firing on the Queen and her troops.

"Oh, no ... we gotta do something, Artoo!" cried the boy. Artoo whistled a reply. The ship's

systems went on and the craft began to levitate. Thanking Artoo, Anakin said, "I'll take over. Let's see ..." Steering the ship at the droids, he pushed a button and the ship began to shake. "Oops, wrong one!"

He found the trigger button and wiped out several droidekas.

The Jedi, engaged in a fierce battle with the Sith Lord, moved into the centre of the hangar. While the droids were distracted by Anakin, Captain Panaka, with Amidala and her troops, managed to reach a palace hallway.

The droidekas fired at Anakin.

"Oops! Shield up!" he exclaimed, flipping several switches and accidentally igniting the after-burner.

The fighter rocketed out of the hangar while Artoo and Anakin held on for dear life.

"Oops! Wrong one!"

The Naboo fleet approached the space station. Trade Federation droid starfighters left the hangars and swarmed near the battleship.

"Enemy fighters straight ahead!" Ric Olié warned his fellow pilots.

A gigantic dogfight ensued.

Anakin's fighter was high over Naboo. The autopilot, searching for other ships aimed at the Trade Federation battleship and the boy found himself right in the middle of the fierce space battle. He saw enemy ships approaching head on.

"Artoo, get us off autopilot!" he cried.

Artoo had been trying to do just that, and he screeched to say he'd succeeded.

"I've got control?" asked Anakin, flipping a switch. "Okay, let's go left!"

Artoo thought they should return to the planet, but Anakin had other ideas. "Qui-Gon told me to stay in this cockpit and that's what I'm gonna do!"

An enemy fighter came into his sights. He tried to fire but activated the wrong control, accelerating his fighter past the enemy ship.

Now it was on his tail. Anakin went into a spin as an evasive measure, making Artoo beep loudly.

"Hang on," said Anakin. "The way out of this mess is the way we got into it."

He yanked on the reverse thrusters, slowing the ship instantly. The enemy fighter shot past and exploded against the space station!

Ric and the spacefighters were attacking the space station, but its deflector shield was too strong.

Meanwhile Anakin was being chased once more. He dodged some parked transport ships, but a huge bulkhead blocked his way. Hitting the reverse thrusters again, the ship skidded to a

halt inside the hangar deck. Artoo gave a worried whistle.

"All right, all right! Get the system started!" said Anakin, ducking down to adjust a control panel. "Everything's overheated. All the lights are on red!"

Artoo saw droids approaching and beeped frantically.

In the Theed palace, Queen Amidala and her group were trapped in a hallway held by battle droids. Panaka blasted a hole in the window and a small group made their way onto a ledge, six storeys above a raging waterfall. From their pistols they fired thin cables which embedded in a window ledge far above them. They climbed up.

Moments later a window in the hallway to the throne room blew apart. Amidala, Panaka, and the soldiers clambered in and made for the door. Two droidekas blocked their path. Two more appeared at the far end of the hallway, trapping them.

Amidala dropped her pistol. "Throw down your weapons," she said.

"But we can't!" argued Captain Panaka.

"Captain, I said throw down your weapons."

Everyone obeyed her strange command.

Amidala, Panaka and half a dozen officers were brought before Nute and Rune, in the throne room.

"Your little insurrection is at an

end, Your Highness," said Nute. "Time for you to sign the treaty."

But then Sabé, dressed like the Queen, appeared in the doorway with several troops. "I will not be signing, viceroy, because you have lost!" she shouted.

Her enemies were stunned. "After her! This one is a decoy!" yelled Nute, indicating the real Queen.

As droids chased after Sabé, Nute turned to Amidala. "Your Queen will not get away with this."

Slumped down on her throne, Amidala hit a security button which opened a panel in her desk. From it, she grabbed two pistols, tossing one to Captain Panaka and one to an officer. She took a third pistol and blasted the remaining battle droids.

The Trade Federation officers rushed to the door control panel as Amidala pressed a switch to close the door. The officer at the door jammed the controls. Captain Panaka threw more pistols to the other guards. The Nemoidians were confused and afraid.

"This is the end of your occupation here," Amidala told the viceroy.

"Don't be absurd," he replied. "It won't be long before hundreds of droidekas break in here to rescue us."

On the grassy plains, Jar Jar's clumsiness was an advantage. He got caught up in the wiring of a battle droid. As he dragged the wrecked droid around with him, its guns still firing he randomly, blasted other droids in the process!

OOM-9 sent hundreds of droidekas rolling out of the transports. They rolled through the deflector shields, then transformed. The Gungans blasted them with energy balls, but, in turn, the droids blasted many Gungans.

The Gungan army was no match for the droidekas and began to retreat. Jar Jar tried to escape on a wagon, but accidentally opened the back gate and sent energy balls rolling downhill — flattening several droids.

At this, the Gungans renewed their attack, and Jar Jar's bumbling destroyed more droidekas. But a droideka blasted one of the generators, and the Gungan shield fell apart. OOM-9 ordered his tanks forward, and the Gungan General signalled a retreat. The Gungans fled in chaos. Some succeeded in fleeing to the hills. Others were herded into groups by battle droids.

Darth Maul's athletic skills were incredible. He was fighting two Jedi at once, flipping into the air and outmanoeuvring them at every turn.

He drove Qui-Gon and Obi-Wan out of the hangar and into a power generator area. The lightsabre blades criss-crossed in an intense struggle. They fought their way across the narrow bridge of the Theed power generator and onto a catwalk. Darth Maul kicked Obi-Wan off a ramp and he fell several levels.

Qui-Gon knocked Darth Maul and caused him to fall two levels before jumping down after him. Darth Maul backed away into a small doorway. Qui-Gon followed him and Obi-Wan ran to catch up.

The Sith Lord entered a long reactor room hallway filled with a series of pulsing, deadly ray walls that cycled on and off.

Darth Maul passed several walls of rays before they cycled on. Qui-Gon was only one wall from him, but Obi-Wan was trapped five walls away.

The Jedi had to wait for the walls to cycle off before they could advance. Obi-Wan paced impatiently; Qui-Gon meditated; and Darth Maul just waited.

The ray walls disappeared. Obi-Wan ran towards Qui-Gon, who was already fighting ferociously with Darth Maul. The two of them had battled their way to the reactor's melting-pit!

The electron ray walls closed, suddenly trapping Obi-Wan and leaving him helpless to assist his Master. He watched, frustrated, as Qui-Gon and Darth Maul battled around the deep

hole of the melting-pit.

Suddenly the Sith Lord caught Qui-Gon off-guard. Darth Maul slammed his lightsabre handle into Qui-Gon's chin before running him through with the blade. The Jedi slumped to the floor in a heap.

The pulsing electron gate opened and Darth Maul began a relentless assault on Obi-Wan.

Catching the tiring young Jedi off-guard Darth Maul lunged and Obi-Wan slipped into the melting-pit and dropped his weapon. He struggled to hold on to a nozzle on the side of the pit. Darth Maul grinned evilly as he kicked his opponent's lightsabre down the bottomless shaft.

At the last moment Obi-Wan jumped out of the pit and summoned the Force to bring Qui-Gon's lightsabre to him. He swung with a vengeance, cutting the Sith down. Darth Maul fell into the melting-pit to his death!

Obi-Wan ran to Qui-Gon. "Master! Master!"

"It is too late ..."

"No!"

"Obi-Wan, promise me you'll train the boy."

"Yes, Master."

"He is the chosen one ... he will bring balance... train him!"

And then ... Qui-Gon died, cradled in the weeping Obi-Wan's arms.

On the battleship hangar deck, Anakin peered over the edge of the cockpit and saw the battle droids surrounding the ship. He ducked down and observed the red lights still on.

"The systems are still overheated, Artoo."

The battle droid captain walked up to the ship and asked where the pilot was. Artoo beeped a reply.

"You're the pilot?" asked the captain. "Let me see your identification."

Anakin saw the dashboard lights had turned green. He flipped a switch and the engine started.

"Come out of there or we'll blast you!" ordered the captain, spotting the boy.

"Not if I can help it! Shields up!" Anakin flipped a switch and the ship levitated, knocking over the battle droid captain.

Anakin fired lasers at the other droids, then shot two torpedoes at them. The torpedoes missed, but flew down a passageway and exploded in the reactor room.

"Let's get out of here!" Anakin shouted.

A moment later his ship roared through the hangar. "Now this is Podracing!"

On the battleship bridge, the Nemoidian was told the reactor was losing power.

"Impossible!" he said — just before the bridge exploded!

Ric Olié watched in amazement from his cockpit as the battleship started to explode from the inside out.

"What's that!?" asked Bravo Two.

"I don't know," said Ric. "We didn't hit it."

At the same moment the droids on the Naboo plain began to shake, they ran in circles, then stopped, as if frozen.

Jar Jar pushed a battle droid and it fell over. "Weirding!" he exclaimed. The droids had been deactivated.

Anakin and Artoo followed the squad of Naboo starfighters back home to the main hangar. Ric and the other pilots climbed out and gathered together in excitement.

"He flew into the hold behind the deflector shield and blasted the main reactor!" said Bravo Two.

"Amazing! They don't teach that at the Academy," replied Bravo Three.

Anakin's ship skidded to a halt. The pilots and ground crew rushed over.

"Who flew the ship?" asked Ric.

Everyone stared in astonishment when the cockpit opened and the small boy stood up.

"I'm not going to get into trouble, am I?" asked Anakin.

The grand cruiser of the Supreme Chancellor landed in the courtyard, Nute and Rune were under guard.

"Now, Viceroy, you are going to have to go back to the Senate and explain all this," said Queen Amidala.

"You can kiss your trade franchise goodbye!" added Captain Panaka.

The main ramp of the cruiser was lowered. Obi-Wan and Captain Panaka led the viceroy and his assistant on board. Palpatine — now Supreme Chancellor — and several Republic guards descended the walkway, followed by Yoda and other Jedi Masters.

"Congratulations on your election, Chancellor," greeted the Queen. "It is so good to see you again."

"It's good to be home," said Palpatine. "Your boldness has saved our people. Together we shall bring peace to the Republic."

It was late in the day, and the sun streamed in through a multi-windowed

turret room in the Jedi Temple. Yoda paced before Obi-Wan, who kneeled in the centre of the room.

"Confer on you, the level of Jedi Knight the Council does," said Yoda. "But agree with your taking this boy as your Padawan learner, I do not."

"Qui-Gon believed in him," replied Obi-Wan. "I believe in Qui-Gon."

"The chosen one, the boy may be; nevertheless, grave danger I fear in his training."

"Master Yoda, I gave Qui-Gon my word. I will train Anakin."

"Qui-Gon's defiance I sense in you. Agree, the Council does. Your apprentice, young Skywalker will be."

Everyone gathered on the funeral temple steps at sunset and watched Qui-Gon's robe go up in flames. There was a drum-roll. Doves were released. And then the Jedi was gone.

"He is one with the Force. You must let go," Obi-Wan told Anakin. "I am your Master now. You will become a Jedi, I promise."

Mace Windu spoke in confidence to Yoda. "There is no doubt. The mysterious warrior was a Sith."

"Always two there are," said Yoda. "A Master and an apprentice."

"But which one was destroyed?" asked Mace. "Master or apprentice?"

The two Jedi Masters looked at one another with deep concern.

The phantom menace had been suppressed and peace reigned once more. The Republic had a new leader, and friendship had been established between the Gungans and Queen Amidala and her people.

Queen Amidala stood with Supreme Chancellor Palpatine, Anakin, Obi-Wan, Sio Bibble, and the Jedi Council.

In the colourful parade that followed, the Gungans stopped before the Queen and walked up the steps to stand by her side.

The end?

STAR WARS
EPISODE I
THE PHANTOM MENACE